Power Play

Power Play

T. E. Walters

Writers Club Press
San Jose New York Lincoln Shanghai

Power Play

All Rights Reserved © 2000 by T. E. Walters

No part of this book may be reproduced or transmitted in any form or by any means, graphic, electronic, or mechanical, including photocopying, recording, taping, or by any information storage retrieval system, without the permission in writing from the publisher.

Writers Club Press
an imprint of iUniverse.com, Inc.

For information address:
iUniverse.com, Inc.
620 North 48th Street, Suite 201
Lincoln, NE 68504-3467
www.iuniverse.com

ISBN: 0-595-09876-2

Printed in the United States of America

Chapter 1

High Sticking

Trevor raced to the corner to grab the puck as his teammates skated to keep up with him. He was the first to reach the puck, and with a whirl of his body, he pivoted and began to race toward the net. He faked left and skated hard to the right. In a flash, he saw that the upper left corner of the net was open. He shot. Nothing but the back of the net!

His team surrounded him, giving him a barrage of pats on his helmet. "Way to go Trev!" they screamed. "Awwwwwesome," cried Al, his best friend. "O.K. guys, we're only down one goal, we've got to get back into this game. Let's go!!" shouted Trev. Everyone on the team gave a battle cry and skated away.

The two skated to the bench so the next line could take their shift. Trevor and Al were always together. At home, at school, and on the rink, the two were completely inseparable.

"These guys are a lot tougher than I thought they were going to be," Al said as he took his spot on the bench.

"I know, they are really physical," replied Trevor. "I just hope we can score one more goal."

Al quickly shot back, "No problem, we'll get 'em next shift."

In Minnesota, youth hockey is split into different levels ranging from Mighty Mites for the youngest to Bantams for the oldest. Beyond that, it's big time high school hockey. The Laketon Bobcats, Al and Trevor's team were in the Squirt League. They were ranked as the number one Squirt team in the state. The Laketon high school team seemed to have a permanent spot in the state tournament, so this area was renowned for its hockey. Most of the top skaters would eventually play for Laketon High. This group of Squirts had skated together since they were Mighty Mites, so they all knew how one another skated. Trevor Eubanks and Al Pilot were the two so called "stars" of the team. They were also the best of friends.

Both had dreams of someday playing professional hockey for the Minnesota Express. Trevor's dad had been one of the team's biggest stars ever, and he was thought of as a true sports hero by nearly everyone in Minnesota. Al's father was a great skater through college but unfortunately blew out his knee in his final game as a collegiate. He too probably could have skated professionally.

This was only the fifth game of the season, but there were already high expectations for this team. Everyone they played came at them with their best game because they were supposedly playing the best team in the state. Most of the time the games were not very close. Usually by the third period, the Bobcats were up by at least five goals.

This game was different though. River Place always had a good team, and they had kind of developed into the arch rivals of the Bobcats. Laketon always prided itself on it's strong passing attack as well as it's superb skating skills. The River Place Tigers were much bigger kids who liked a more physical style. It usually made for an interesting game.

Just as Al and Trev were getting comfortable on the bench, Zeke Bowden from the Tigers stole the puck and started down the ice on a breakaway.

"C'mon guys! You've gotta stop him!!" screeched Trevor.

"Let's go Toby! You can STOP him!" Al chimed in.

In the stands there was very little noise as Zeke took his stick back and quickly made a powerful stroke. The puck went flying. Toby, the goaltender, slid to his right to block the shot but missed the puck entirely.

"CCCCCLLLLAAAANNNNNGGGGG." The puck hit the post and bounced to the boards. A Bobcat skated into the corner and cleared the puck out of their zone. That signaled a line shift as Trevor and Al quickly scrambled back onto the ice.

"That was WAY too close," Al shouted to Toby as he skated by the net.

"I know, we have to be more careful with the puck," replied Toby. " You guys are hanging me out to dry here!"

"Calm down Toby; we'll get this game tied up in a minute," assured Trevor. The Bobcats had regained control of the puck and were passing it forward toward the River Place side. The two teams skated back and forth for a few minutes before Al made a perfect pass to Trevor by the blue line. Trev faked out the defenseman and made a dash for the goal.

The River Place goalie skated out to cut down the angle of Trevor's shot. Trev pretended to shoot. The goalie went down on his knees to block the shot as Trev scooped the puck up in the air just enough to make it over the goalie's outstretched glove. The puck fell slowly into the net. The score was now tied up at four goals apiece.

The crowd cheered loudly as Trev pumped his fists. "YEAAAAHHH!" he screamed. "I knew we could do it! Now come on guys, let's show these bullies how we can skate!" he continued.

Time was ticking down; there were only three minutes left in the third period. Both teams were concentrating on playing good defense. There hadn't been a shot on goal in the last ten minutes of the game. It was now time for one of the teams to step up and finish off the game. This game had definitely been a much tougher test than Laketon had anticipated.

Al skated into the far corner to retrieve the puck. He met up with Zeke from River Place, and the two began to exchange words.

"You guys are just a bunch of sissies!" Zeke yelled.

Power Play

"Maybe, but we're still going to beat you guys," Al shouted back. And with that, he took the puck away from Zeke and began to skate toward the opponents net. Zeke, obviously frustrated, brought his stick up and hit Al on his face mask. The whistle blew.

"High sticking on number 29, gold!" shouted the referee.

So, with under a minute to play, the Bobcats had their fourth power play of the game. They had been practicing their power play passing extremely hard the past week, so they felt confident about scoring.

As Trevor took the face off the voice of his father could be heard through the crowd. "Skate hard, Trev!" he screamed. The referee dropped the puck and Trev passed it back to his defenseman, Nathan. The Bobcats entered the Tigers' zone and kept the puck moving.

The clock just kept ticking. Ten, nine, eight, seven. Trevor flashed in front of the net just as Al passed the puck. Four, three, two. With a flick of his wrist he set the puck toward the net. The Tigers' goalie wasn't prepared to stop the puck, and as time ran out, the puck crossed the line. Final score Bobcats 5 Tigers 4.

Chapter 2

The Ride Home

The team was celebrating in the locker room as Trevor and Al made their way to the nearest bench. Before the season began, the team had decided their main goal of the year was to go undefeated and become the State Squirt Champions. The victory over the Tigers put the Bobcats at 5-0. The rest of the games probably wouldn't be quite this difficult, but they did have the season finale at River Place.

"Man, those guys were tough!" exclaimed Trevor.

"I know. I hope we can improve a little by the time we face up with them again," replied Al.

"You know what Al?" asked Trevor. "Our defense needs to get a lot better or else there is no way we can finish the year undefeated."

"Shut up Trevor. We just had an off game, O.K.?"

The two continued to change out of their uniforms. "Nice hat trick Trev!" shouted Andrew, the team jokester. The team could always count on Andrew to keep things somewhat light and humorous.

"Hey, thanks man," Trevor replied as he playfully punched Andrew on the shoulder.

After five games, this was Trev's third three goal game. Of course hat tricks and Trevor had become synonymous lately. Looking back over the past two years of hockey Al could not remember a game where

Trevor didn't score at least one goal. The kid was amazing, and Al looked up to his best friend almost as an idol.

"Hey Al, can I catch a ride home with you guys?" Trevor asked. "My dad said he had to catch up with some work at his office. He told me to catch a ride with you guys."

"Sure, but you know my dad is going to be there, don't you? You sure you still want a ride?" asked Al. His father was notorious for going over every single detail of each game on the ride home. Trevor avoided getting a ride with Al as much as possible. He probably didn't mean to be so annoying, but talking about hockey right after a tough game wasn't the topic the kids usually felt like discussing. They would probably rather talk about video games or the latest must-see movie.

"That's all right; we'll just try to get him to talk about his old college days or something," replied Trevor.

They finished dressing and gave the coach a high five on the way out of the locker room. Jeff Pilot, Al's dad, was waiting for them by the concession stands. He was in the middle of a group of parents complaining about how bad the officiating was and how they should play the best line for more of each game. "I know this is just Squirts, but if that coach wants to win a title, he's got to learn that the best skaters need to be on the ice for **most** of the game-especially in the last period," Mr. Pilot told another parent. Before he could embarrass Al, Trevor walked up to Mr. Pilot and tapped him on the shoulder.

"Hey Mr. P, can I catch a ride with you guys, my dad kind of took off on me?"

"Well, well, well. If it isn't "Mr. Hat trick,"" Mr. Pilot teased as he tousled Trevor's hair. "Sure Trevor, why don't you guys go get your gear and put it in the trunk. I'll be right out."

Trevor caught the car keys in mid air and turned to get Al. The two then picked up their overstuffed gear bags and headed to the parking lot. On the way out Zeke walked past them with a huge scowl on his face. "Boy he does not looked pleased," kidded Trevor.

"I know, it looks like he just lost his best friend," replied Al. They both looked at each other and started to laugh, as they ran out to the parking lot to load up the truck. They got inside and turned the radio to KZBA, the coolest station in town (or at least that's what Trevor and Al liked to think). They played all the latest music and everyone at school listened to it too.

After about five minutes, Mr. Pilot jumped into the driver's seat. "Turn this junk off," he began, "I can't even hear myself think." With a quick twist of his wrist the radio became silent.

Al gave Trev a funny look, as if to say, "I can't help it."

"You boys should feel pretty lucky after that dismal display of hockey!" Mr. Pilot started. "Al, it looked like you were confused out there or something. Why did you allow that kid from River Place to go right by you for that last goal?"

"B-b-but dad, I didn't"

"Don't interrupt me son. I'm not trying to be hard on you. I just want to see you become the best hockey player that you can. Don't you realize that after all these years?" replied Mr. Pilot.

"I understand that dad. I just don't feel like talking about the game right now."

Trevor hated to see Mr. Pilot take out all of his frustrations in front of him, so he decided it was probably time to intervene. "Hey Mr. P, when you played for the Badgers did you guys ever get to play against Harvard?"

"We only played them once. In the NCAA tourney," Mr.Pilot said as he began to perk up. "It was the Final Four right here in St. Paul. They were the defending national champs, and we were about a three goal underdog. However, the pregame speech from our coach really got us pumped up. Let me see. I think the speech was something like this…" Mr. Pilot was in his own world now. Trevor knew that bringing up his college playing days would always get Mr. Pilot to change the subject. The rest of the ride home involved listening to the infamous story about

Harvard and the "biggest game in Badger history," as Mr. P liked to describe it.

"Thanks for the ride Mr. P," Trev said as he jumped out of the truck.

"Anytime, big guy."

"Hey Al, give me a call tomorrow. Maybe we can go to the lake with the guys to play a little pond hockey?" Trevor suggested.

"Yeah, I'll give ya a ring. See ya."

Trevor shut the door and watched as the Pilots pulled out of his driveway. He shook his head and moved toward the front door. Trevor was extremely thankful that his dad didn't go overboard about hockey. Even though he was once a professional hockey player, his dad never really pushed him as far as hockey was concerned.

Chapter 3

Pond Hockey

The best thing about pond hockey is that there are no parents, coaches, or undo pressure. It's just ten to twelve kids skating to their own rules and just having fun. Minnesota has the reputation of being a haven for hockey. Sometimes the pressures that go along with top-notch hockey can become too great. Since there are over 10,000 lakes in the state, pond hockey becomes a sort of refuge from organized competitive hockey.

It was the perfect early December day-about 27 degrees and sunny. The cool, crisp air along with the faint smell of fireplaces hard at work made the conditions ideal for hockey. The only downside of pond hockey was that there was no Zamboni machine to clear the ice. The players had to bring their shovels in order to clear the rink each time. This usually took about a half hour. After that came the ritual of choosing teams. Trevor was always one of the captains. If he got the first choice, everyone there knew he would pick Al, unless Al was a captain as well.

Today, that didn't happen. Jeff was the other captain and picked Al first. Trev quickly picked Toby so that he would be sure to get the best goalie. Usually the teams were pretty equal, so the games were always close. They were high scoring games which meant a good goalie could prove to be the difference. A typical game would usually end with a score of about 17 to 15. A real defensive struggle.

The games always began with one team starting at their own net since there were no referees to drop the puck for a face-off. The rules were slightly different as well. The games were much rougher than a normal Squirt game because they liked to play as if they were in the NHL. Trevor shined in these types of games even more than he did in organized hockey due to his superior skating skills. Everyone just knew that he would follow in his father's footsteps and turn pro.

The game started and Trevor immediately took the puck and headed toward the other side of the pond. Al knew all of Trev's moves, so he skated right at him. He planned on trying to check him. Just as Al was about to hit Trevor, one of Trev's teammates blind sided him from the left. Trev kept skating. He deeked out the two defensemen with his patented spin move, and suddenly he was one on one with Nate, the opposing goalie. Instead of shooting, Trev spun and pretended to skate the other way. Just as he was all the way turned around, he flipped the puck back straight through Nate's legs.

"One-zip!" shouted Trev.

"You choke, ya bum!" yelled Al. "I was about to deck you when Jeff blind sided me."

"You better watch where you skate," replied Trevor with a huge smile.

After one hour, the score was 11-7 in favor of Al's team. They decided to take a break from the action. They usually broke the game into halves of about an hour each instead of the traditional three periods. The first hour was wide open, but the second hour was usually much more physical and lower scoring. Usually, but not today.

"I can't believe we're down four goals," Trevor said tiredly, as they sat at the edge of the pond catching their breath. "Man I need to rest."

"What's the matter? Score too many goals yesterday?" mocked Al.

"Shut up. I just can't seem to get into the flow today," replied Trevor.

So far that afternoon, Al had scored three goals and Trev only had the opening one. "Maybe you just lost your touch," said Nate as he skated up to the "dynamic duo." "I know I'm a good goalie, but I never knew that I was this good."

Trevor shot back, "Hey give me a break Nate. You don't have to skate every day! You should be well rested because you never even play for the Bobcats!"

Nate's insides turned red hot. He hated sitting on the bench. Each game he wished he could be out on the ice with his buddies. Finally that anger had welled up too long and he burst out, "I bet you don't score for the rest of the day, dufus!"

"You're on, but you will be sorry," smiled Trevor. "Whoever loses the bet has to carry the other's books at school for two weeks." Motivation usually was not a factor with Trevor, but when there was a challenge, he was ready and willing to step up and accept.

"You bet, let's go," Nate replied.

"Wait a minute man, I've got to catch my breath," gasped Trevor. Nate skated away and began to crease ready for action.

"What got into Nate?" Trevor asked Al.

"He thinks you don't like him since you always pick Toby before him," said Al.

"Well, Toby's the better goalie. What does he think, I want to lose or something?"

Al stuck up for his fellow teammate by saying, "Keep talking big guy, and I will make sure that you don't score again today." Al smugly threatened as he skated away.

"Just watch this," Trevor muttered to himself. Trevor skated to his teammates and said, "O.K. guys, I just received a little challenge. They bet me I couldn't score the rest of the day. Well we're down by four goals, and I want to prove them wrong. Can you guys keep them off my back and concentrate on defense? I want to score the rest of our goals. I promise that the next game on this pond we will ask for a rematch. I'll let you guys score all the goals and we will still kick their butts. Who's with me?"

Everyone screamed "YEAH!" as they rushed back to the ice.

The tension could have been cut with a pair of scissors as Trevor's team began the second half with the puck. Trevor's team was out for vengeance. They were skating hard and fast. Within three minutes, Trevor had his first goal on a hard slap shot from the left of the net.

"There goes your bet Nate!" Trev shouted as he skated by. "That's just the beginning. You ain't seen nothing yet."

Trevor's second goal came about five minutes later after a beautiful pass from Jeff.

"Two down and two to go!" yelled Trev.

Toby wasn't going to back down. Not now. "That's it man. You ain't gettin no more on me!" The talk was tough, but inside there was a doubt that was beginning to well up a bit.

The third and fourth goals came on end to end streaks by Trevor. That tied the score at 11, and Trevor now had five goals. He was not even close to being finished

Trevor scored thee more goals before the afternoon was over. With the score 14-11 and with only one shot on goal in the second half , Al's team decided the game was over.

"**Time out!**" Al shouted. "I think we got your message; that's enough for today!"

Trevor celebrated for a few minutes with his team before skating over to Nate. "Hey Nate, I think you are a great goalie. I just didn't like the challenge, you know. Keep working and you will see a lot of action before the season is over," Trevor said.

"Yeah, I guess so. I think I learned a lesson today," replied Nate. "But you just wait…all I need are a few more practices."

"Keep up the hard work, Nate. You'll get there" Trevor said as he patted Nate on the back.

"Thanks man."

The walk home with Al was pretty quiet. Neither spoke to each other until they reached Al's house.

"Hey, great game Trev. You are awesome."

"Shut up, you are just as good. Hey, I'll see ya tomorrow at school," replied Trevor as he turned and headed toward his house.

As Al watched Trevor walk away, he stared in amazement. "I can't believe he scored seven straight goals," he thought to himself. "He is definitely going to be a star someday."

Chapter 4

Pressure

"So, how did the big game go?" asked Jo Beth, Al's mother.

"It was okay. We lost by three goals. You should have seen Trevor. I've never seen anyone skate so well," replied Al.

"What do you mean?"

"Well, we were up 11 to 7 at break when Nate decided to challenge Trev. Anyway, it came down to a bet that Trev wouldn't score the rest of the game. That kind of turned into a bad idea. A very bad idea!"

"So what did Trevor do?" asked Jo Beth.

"He scored seven straight goals and we lost 14-11." Al's mother began to laugh.

"Well I guess that taught you guys a lesson or two."

"I know, I know," Al said. "I just wish I could be a as good as Trev, you know."

"Your father seems to think you can."

"Yeah, he thinks that if I practice 2000 hours a week I will turn out to be a superstar. Hey, by the way, where is dad?"

"He's down in the basement watching T.V."

Al snatched up three cookies on the counter and headed downstairs. He wanted to know what was going on, and tell his dad about Trevor's exploits on the pond.

"Hey dad, whatcha watchin?"

"How are you? How did the game go?"

"It was a great game, but we lost by three goals."

"Was Trevor on your team?"

The T.V. suddenly blared as one of the Gophers scored a basket to go up by two points in their Big Ten opening game. There were quite a few who believed the Gophers might actually win the Big Ten basketball championship this season.

"No, is this the Gopher game?" Al said wondering if bringing up the subject of hockey was the brightest thing to do at that moment. That usually meant a lecture on the finer points of hockey and competition. Somewhere along the line Jeff Pilot began to believe that his son, Al, would be the next great hockey player to come out of Minnesota. Whether or not it was true, it still put an enormous amount of pressure on Al. He constantly had to live up to the extremely high expectations of his father.

"You bet, they have been playing really well today. They just scored so I think they're up by two on Iowa," said Mr. Pilot.

"Cool. See I told you they were going to be contenders this year."

"That you did. That you did. So, what made the hockey game so exciting?"

Al told the story all over again with most of the details intact. He noticed his father becoming more and more interested. When he finally finished with the story his dad took a deep breath. Al knew what was coming.

"Wow, that kid can play can't he?" Mr. Pilot asked rhetorically.

"Yeah, he's awesome," Al said. "I wish that I had those skating skills."

"I do NOT want to hear that excuse again." Jeff was beginning to get hot under the collar. "I never had those God given talents, but look where all of my hard work got me. I was on a National Championship team and would have gone pro if my knee hadn't quit on me. You have that same ability that I had. If you work hard, you **will** make it!"

"I know dad." Sometimes Al wished he never had started playing hockey. If he had chosen basketball instead, maybe his father would be more normal. But he had decided to skate. At first it was great, but the pressures began to mount as Al got older. It was almost to a point where he couldn't take it anymore. Al loved the sport of hockey, but the pressure…he could do without.

"You know that I'm available to help you out with any questions you have about the game, don't you son?"

"Yeah, but…" Al began.

"But what?"

"Nothing, let's just watch the end of the Gopher game." Al so desperately wanted to tell his dad that he was suffocating him. He just wanted to have a normal childhood like everyone else. The NHL could wait.

"I can't believe that he scored seven goals in a row!" Jeff Pilot said as they turned toward the t.v.. "I've never seen anybody score like that. He's going to be just like his father, dominating!"

The game ended with the Gophers on top, and Al headed for his room. He still had not eaten the cookies he had picked up earlier. He just did not feel like eating right now. He set the cookies on his desk, jumped on his bed, and picked up a tube that had some of his pog collection in it.

Al's sister, Theresa, didn't know how much easier she had it than him. There were no expectations placed on her. She did well in school, and that's all that their parents cared about. "I wish she played hockey," Al thought. "If only she would join one of those new girl leagues. Then maybe she could find out what it means to play under pressure." Al knew deep down that even that wouldn't be the same.

Al would sometimes spend hours upon hours in his room just so he wouldn't have to talk "hockey" with his father. Usually he would read a magazine or look at his pog collection. Today he felt like just laying on his bed, so he threw his pogs back on the floor and laid their in silence. "There had to be a way out of this pressure," he thought to himself. After about ten minutes, Al fell asleep. His sister had to come in and wake him up for dinner.

Chapter 5

Time Out!

The Bobcats had now run their record to 16-0. It was the week after Christmas, and because of their record, the team had qualified for the prestigious Toronto Cup Tournament. All of the best squirt teams from around Canada and Minnesota were invited to compete. This was the first year since 1983 that a team from Laketon actually qualified. Needless to say, the players, parents, and coaches were all excited.

The traveling expenses for each player was nearly $1,000. They had spent the last two weeks selling candy bars all across town trying to raise enough money so they could play. Most of the kids on the team raised about half of the money, the rest was paid by their parents. The amount of money that a hockey parent spends in a year is staggering. Some spend close to ten thousand dollars on equipment, ice time, meals, gas, places to stay, and sometimes airfare. This was one expensive trip they didn't mind paying for.

The team flew to Toronto on December 28, just three days after Christmas. The games started on Thursday, the next day, so the team spent most of their spare time watching movies and playing video games at the hotel. Staying in your own room with one other player from the team was the coolest thing about these tournaments. The two compadres naturally roomed together. Nervousness led to a fairly calm first night at the hotel.

On the bus ride to the ice rink the next day, they had the chance to see the sights of Toronto. The huge CN Tower(it looked like a huge space needle) and the Skydome were the obvious favorites. When they arrived at the arena, every single player's jaw dropped. This was bigger than any rink they had skated in before. In fact, it was probably twice as big as anything they had previously skated in back in Minnesota.

"WOW, I can't believe the size of this sucker!" Toby shouted.

Al nudged Trevor and said, "I thought Minnesota was hockey crazy, but these people REALLY take their hockey seriously." Trevor chuckled, but deep down he could feel those butterflies starting to turn inside his stomach.

The inside of the arena was even more impressive. There were stands completely surrounding the ice rink, and they weren't bleachers. They were actual seats, just like any professional arena. No one really knew, but they guessed that the arena probably seated seven or eight thousand people. The concession stand area was enormous. Most of their parents were waiting there, cheering them on as they moved toward the locker room.

Once in the locker room, they realized that this was the "big time." Each player had an open locker that stretched from the floor to the ceiling. The entire place was carpeted as well. In front of each locker, there was a blue plastic chair for each player.

"This place is a regular Taj Mahal," said Toby.

"What is a Taj Mahal?" inquired Nathan.

"Who cares guys," started Trevor, "let's just get ready for our game, O.K.?"

Every player from each team was introduced before the first game of the tournament. They skated out to the blue line and made a quick stop so little slivers of ice flew into the air. It didn't mean much to the game but everyone on the team thought it made them look like a pro team.

The opposing team was from somewhere in Saskatchewan, Canada called Melfort. The first five minutes of the game were fairly boring because both teams were trying to get a feel for the other team's game. There was no real threat of scoring from either team. That was until number 23 from Melfort stole a lazy pass from Trevor to Al. With the puck, he quickly skated into Bobcat territory until he and Toby were alone. It was over before the crowd could react. Number 23 had slammed the puck past Toby in the blink of an eye.

While the other team celebrated, Trevor skated up to Toby and said, "That was totally my fault. I should never have tried to pass the puck like that. It was a sloppy mistake."

He then hit Toby's goal stick with his and skated to the bench as if to say, "it won't happen again." The rest of the period went without a goal from either side and ended 1-0 in favor of Melfort. The Bobcats skated to the edge of the rink with their heads down.

During the intermission, their coach told them this was still anyone's game. "It was a fluke goal, guys. We usually don't make mistakes like that. We'll get it back this period." After the adrenalizing pep talk, the players returned to the ice with renewed vigor.

The second period started well for the Bobcats. They pretty much controlled the puck for the first seven minutes of the period. Melfort's goalie was up to the challenge though, and stopped at least six good shots on goal from Laketon. Trevor and Al began to get a little tired. Instead of skating hard to every loose puck, they were both hoping one of their teammates would get to it. This had a negative effect on the rest of the team. Soon, they all looked out of sync.

Melfort took advantage of it and began to put more pressure on them. Before the period was over, they had added another goal and led 2-0 at the break.

The coach was not as friendly, or as encouraging, during the second intermission. He let them have it in the locker room. It was perfectly clear that they were not skating up to their ability.

The third period face-off was won by Melfort. Their attack was in high gear now. They knew that one more goal and that would be just about it for Laketon.

With crisp, quick passing, they moved into the Bobcat's zone. Five passes later and the score was 3-0.

"TIME OUT!!!" screamed their coach.

Time outs at the beginning of the third period were very unusual. They were usually saved for the end of the game and last minute strategy. But, something needed to be done to get the team on the right track again.

"I'm only going to say this once, so listen up," the coach began. "I want each one of you to look up into the stands. See your parents? They did not spend thousands of dollars to see you guys come here and play like a bunch of sissies. You're playing like you don't deserve to be here. We were invited to this thing for a reason. We are a GREAT team! Do you understand that? Now, lets play like a GREAT team for the rest of the period and show them how we play hockey in Minnesota!"

The team huddled and made their cheer, "BOBCATS!" Trevor winked to Al as if to tell him that it was time for some magic. The two skated to center ice for the face-off.

Before the face-off, Trevor turned to his team and said, "Let's show 'em how to play some pond hockey!" Toby, and the rest of the team smiled. They knew it was time to turn up the intensity.

Trevor took the face-off, spun around, and began to weave in and out of Melfort's defense like it was Swiss cheese. His puck handling was impeccable as he moved toward the net. Just as Melfort began to crash down upon him, he dumped the puck off to Al who swiped at the puck. The puck sailed into the back of the net.

The momentum of the game was beginning to shift.

Two more minutes passed. Trevor broke free along the boards, and Nathan made a perfect pass just as Trev crossed the blue line. Trevor was one-on-one with the other goalie now. He skated hard down the right side straight at the goal. He faked a shot, swooped behind the net, and dumped the puck across the goal line as the goalie lay sprawled on the ice. The crowd went wild. It had been a while since they had seen such inspired hockey.

Trevor played the entire third period without a break. He ended up with two goals and three assists as Laketon squeaked out a 5-3 win. Gordie Eubanks was the first onto the ice after the game. He gave his son a huge hug and a high five. Al looked for his father, but he was nowhere to be seen.

He skated over to Trevor and his dad. "Hey Mr. Eubanks, have you seen my dad?"

Mr. Eubanks slid over to Al and gave him a hug too. "Great game Al, you guys looked awesome that last period."

"Thanks, have you seen my dad?"

"Oh, uh, I think he left after Melfort went up 3-0. I guess he thought it was over. He said something about going back to the hotel. He seemed kind of upset."

"Thanks," said Al dejectedly. He desperately wanted to celebrate this win with his father too. Instead he skated slowly toward the locker room.

Chapter 6

School Heroes

The Monday morning bus ride to school was more exciting than most. Both Trevor and Al were overcome with excitement. They couldn't wait to tell everyone at school how their tournament had gone. After the close call with a tough Melfort team, Laketon had swept their remaining three games easily. None of the games were even close. The championship game's final score was Laketon 7, Stevens West 2. Trevor, as usual, was simply amazing. In four games he had scored 14 goals and had 9 assists. When the time came for the MVP award to be presented, there was absolutely no doubt who would win.

"Man that was just so cool. I can't think of anything that could be as exciting as beating those guys from Canada in Toronto!" exclaimed Al. "You were boss man. Nobody came close to stopping you."

"Hey, it was a team effort. Without you guys to pass to, we probably would have lost all of our games," replied Trevor. "Besides, you and Toby were named to the All-Tourney team too!"

"I know, I can't believe it. I can't wait to tell Mr. Winslow. He didn't think we would do too well up there. Well, we showed him." With that, the dynamic duo turned and gave each other a high five. Mr. Winslow was their fourth grade teacher. Both of the boys thought he was the best teacher they ever had, or will ever have. Of course it wasn't his teaching they liked about him. Mr. Winslow was a huge sports fan too, so they enjoyed talking about hockey and other sports with him.

They seemed to have a friendly sort of competition amongst them, so they figured they would rub it in when the first bell rang. The bus pulled up slowly to the curb at school. While they were gone, Minnesota had received a huge dumping of white fluffy snow. There was a fresh five inches that blanketed the ground. Trevor reached down, packed a snowball, and turned to heave one at Al. He was too late. Al was already at the doors.

"Man, he really wants to talk to Winslow," Trev muttered to himself. He dropped his snowball and headed towards his classroom.

Once inside, the hectic chaos that every Monday morning at any school brings was in full swing. Kids were everywhere. Some were fighting for a good spot to hang their stuff, some were talking about their weekend, some were already beginning to poke and prod each other, and some were actually getting ready for the day. Most of the teachers were busily preparing for the day in their rooms. Mr. Winslow, however, was not doing the same. Al had him trapped by the door already and was laying into him about how great his hockey team was. Trevor nodded to Mr. Winslow on the way to his seat.

"Hey wait a minute Trevor; I heard you were pretty miraculous up there in Canada?" Mr. Winslow bellowed interrupting Al's monologue.

"Yeah, well we did well I guess."

"What do you mean "I guess?" Weren't you picked MVP of the tourney?"

"Well yeah but…"

"No buts about it. That's great, congratulations," replied Mr. Winslow.

"Thanks," said Trevor as he finally made it to his seat. Al immediately began to kid with Mr. Winslow about how he didn't know anything about hockey. That was the great thing about Mr. W; he always had time to talk with them. Everyone thought that was very cool.

An interesting feature at Ridgeway Elementary was that every single classroom has a television set. Important school info was constantly being shown on channel 19 every single day. Also, every morning the entire school watched the announcements at the same time. Usually a group of about five students read some of the daily news after the National anthem was played and the students had recited the Pledge of Allegiance. Overall, it was a lot better than listening to a teacher drone on about the days events.

Everything was going along as always when Trevor heard his name. The person reading the announcements today just happened to be Amy Swift. Now that might not mean much to any of you, but she perhaps had the world's largest crush on a certain star hockey player. Trevor's face began to turn as red as the Nebraska Cornhusker sweatshirt he was wearing. Trevor kind of liked Amy too, but he was just too busy with hockey and school to worry about girls right now. He really didn't want it to distract him from his hockey.

Everyone watched the television as Amy reported on how well the Bobcats had done in the Toronto tournament. She went on to talk about how well certain players had played and finished with news that Trevor had been named MVP of the tourney. She actually had an old newspaper clipping of Trevor's that the camera quickly zoomed in on for a close up! All of the eyes in the classroom turned to Trevor as he buried himself in his arms.

"Well we should all congratulate our scholar athletes on a job well done this past weekend," Mr. Winslow bellowed as he stood up and lead a raucous round of applause. After that, things quieted down. They could now concentrate on school, at least some of them could. Trevor hadn't quite gotten over his embarrassing situation. At recess Mr. Winslow stopped Trevor and asked him how he liked the attention that morning.

"You mean that YOU arranged that little broadcast?" Trevor asked.

"Sure, I saw how well you guys did in this morning's paper, so I decided to have Amy make a little presentation."

"You would have to pick her," Trevor said as he hung his head.

" What do you mean? Oh, I get it. She likes you, doesn't she?" uttered Mr. Winslow in a slightly sarcastic tone.

"Funny. Real funny," Trevor replied along with a little jab to Mr. W's arm.

The remainder of the day went well, except for the constant joking that Trevor's friends gave him. He was pretty used to it, and was able to shrug most of it off to silliness. The only things in life that really mattered to Trevor right now were hockey and doing well in school. The same could not be said for Al. Girls had become a big part of his life. He was constantly talking about them. One, in particular, really sparked his interest…Jenny Baxter.

Chapter 7

No Girls Allowed

A couple of weeks later, Trev and Al were sitting around in Al's room when the subject of girls came up once again. "Trevor, would you ever consider going on a date with someone this year?" Al asked inquisitively.

"No, I really don't feel like it yet," Trev replied.

"What if she was really cute, you know, like Amy Swift?"

"Shut up Al," Trevor quickly blurted, and grabbed one of Al's comic books to read. Al had about a zillion comic books, or at least it seemed like he had that many. Most of them were action hero comics with the good guys triumphing over the evil entities of the universe. Some were really old and kind of corny. Those were the ones that Trevor liked the most. He thought the action ones were all the same. They always had a super hero in some kind of crazy predicament that seemed to be impossible to escape from, and just when you start to think that its all over for this super hero, somehow a magical power appears and "BAM" the good guys triumph once again. So, even though the old ones were kind of corny, Trevor liked to read them the most. At least they were original.

About ten minutes later Al started to talk about the girl situation at school again. "You know who I think is really cute, Trev?"

"Let me guess, uh, uh, Jenny?"

"Yeah, how'd you know?"

"Well it's kind of obvious, you dufus."

Al gave Trevor a sideways glance and went back into deep thought again. It was always fun just to watch Al because you could literally tell exactly what he was thinking. This is just what Trevor was doing at the moment. "What's up Al?"

"What do you mean?"

"I can totally tell that you're thinking of something," Trev replied.

"It's no big deal. Just forget about it, o.k.?"

Sometimes it was hard for Al to let what he was thinking out. It seemed as though he had so much bottled up inside of him. Someday it would catch up to him, and Trevor probably understood that the best. Instead of letting him sit there and sulk, Trevor made Al spill his guts. "This is stupid, Al. Just tell me what's going on."

"It's hard for me to tell you because you're not as into girls as I am."

"So? I still know how you feel. It's about Jenny isn't it?"

"Yeah. And my dad," Al replied. There was a lengthy pause.

"How does your dad have anything to do with Jenny?"

"Well...it's kind of a long story. I'm really interested in going out with Jenny, and I think she knows that. It's just that whenever I call her, my dad ends up getting on the other line and telling me to get back to my schoolwork. It's like living with the police or something. I can't do anything without him getting on my case. And when she calls, forget it. My dad won't even let me talk to her. So she kind of stopped calling."

"Why's your dad so against Jenny?" Trevor asked.

"He's not really against Jenny so much as he's against the whole idea of girls. He thinks that it will somehow affect my skating. He's like a drill sergeant, you know? Every weekend we are out on that stupid pond practicing stick handling, skating techniques, and anything else that has to do with becoming a "*GREAT* " hockey player. After awhile I just get sick of the whole thing."

"Wow. I never knew it was so bad. I mean everyone knows that your dad gets a little intense, but what your saying sounds kind of overboard, don't you think?"

The two sat in silence contemplating what had just been said. Al finally felt slightly relieved to have told someone his problems. Trevor couldn't imagine having that constant pressure placed on him. In a sense, he was lucky his father had lived through that kind of life growing up in Canada. Gordie, Trev's dad, was forced to skate at a very young age. The insane workout schedule made him a great hockey player, but it also took something away from his childhood. Ever since then, he became determined not to let the same thing happen to his son.

"So what are you going to do?" Trevor inquired.

"I have no idea. Jenny's probably really sick of this. At this rate I'm not even going to have a chance of going out with her," Al responded in a dejected voice.

"I think I've got an idea of how this might work," Trev muttered, not quiet sure if he knew what he was talking about.

"Quiet, my sister might be lurking somewhere close by," Al warned.

The two began to whisper about Trev's supposedly clever plan. After about a half an hour, they grabbed their jackets and headed for their secret fort in the woods. They spent the remainder of the day planning and talking about how they could pull off the seemingly impossible. The session finally ended with Trevor saying, "Well I guess we're going to have to abolish the **No Girls Allowed** policy, huh Al?"

"It's up to you Trevor. You're the one who made the stupid policy in the first place."

Trevor knew how into girls Al was, so halfway through the season he came up with the No Girls Allowed idea. The premise was that by avoiding the whole dating scene, the two could focus their energy on something really important, like HOCKEY! The way Al had been acting lately wasn't helping anybody, so he figured the N.G.A. rule should be put on hold for the rest of the season. Their entire plan was based on the fact that if Trevor would ask out Amy, then Mr. Pilot might let Al go on a double date. The only reason Trevor was willing to follow through on their plan was for his friend. He still wasn't all that interested in girls, but if this would help Al out, then he could break his code. They really had faith that this plan would work since Mr. Pilot usually let Al do anything Trevor was doing. Now came the hard part…asking Amy out on a date.

Butterflies are a part of any sport. When game time rolls around, anyone who isn't just a tiny bit nervous usually doesn't play very well. On occasion, some kids took it to the extreme and actually vomited in the locker room before the opening face-off. Neither Trevor nor Al ever got that nervous. However, the next day at school the two were more nervous than they had ever been before any game. It was time to show themselves how courageous they could be. The plan sounded much better last night when they weren't faced with the impending doom of looking into the eyes of a fifth grade girl and asking her out on a date.

Both toyed with the idea of passing a note or letting someone else ask for them, but they figured that was the chicken way out. The entire bus ride to school was uneventful. Usually they were laughing and giggling and telling jokes. Not today. Today, they sat facing the front of the bus with stony expressions on their faces. Not a single word was spoken except for "Hi, how ya doin?" The first bell rang and still the two hadn't made their move. "Let's wait till recess, Al. O.k.?"

"Oh, all right, but I don't want you chickening out on me!" Al responded.

"No, no. I won't."

They went in and sat down at their desks. The morning announcements came and went without anything sinking in. The work that Mr. Winslow assigned in their language books was much too difficult to think about when they had so many other MORE important things on their minds. Time seemed to be at a standstill. Tick, tick, tick. They could actually hear the hands on the clock move. Finally, it was time for recess.

In Minnesota, recess was almost ALWAYS outside. On rare occasions in the winter months, the windchill would reach dangerously cold temps causing the Governor to mandate that kids stay inside during recess. Fortunately the days of Winter this year had been somewhat normal. So outside they headed. Trevor and Al could usually be found playing soccer or messing around with the guys. Not today. Today they stood huddled close the wall getting ready to make their move.

Finally Al nudged Trev, "Come on let's just get it over with."

"O.K. Here we go," Trevor exhaled as he made the first step to the girls.

The main problem they encountered was that the girls were in a group with about seven other girls, so first they needed to go ask if the could talk to Amy and Jenny privately. The butterflies were swarming as they walked towards the girls. As they approached the group, the strangest thing happened. The group of girls actually seemed to get further and further away. It was like one of those creepy science fiction movies they'd seen late on Friday nights.

Finally they made it to the group. "Hey, what's up?"

Most of the girls kind of giggled when they saw who it was interrupting their conversation, which incidentally had been about boys. "Hi guys, what are you two doing here?" asked Amy.

"Well, uh, umm, actually Al and I want to kind of talk to you and Jenny. Privately," Trevor managed to sputter.

Instantly the girls' eyes widened. Everyone in the group focused their attention on the foursome. "Oh. I guess. Sure. Let's go Jenny," Amy replied.

The four walked to the corner of the school which was much less crowded than the rest of the playground. Not a single word was spoken until they reached their destination. On the playground, games stopped and people began to gather and take notice of what was about to happen. Toby asked Jeff what was going on. Jeff had no clue. No one really knew what was going on, although they had a fairly good idea.

"So, what do you guys want anyway?" asked Jenny with a slight smile.

Trevor turned to Amy and said, "Well Al and I, we...uh would uh...like to ask you out on uh...ummm...a date."

Al quickly spoke up to save his stammering friend, "What Mr. Tongue is trying to say is would YOU(pointing at both Amy and Jen) like to go out with US (pointing at himself and Trevor) on Saturday. Maybe we could go to a movie or something?"

There it was, out in the open. A huge sense of relief came over both of the boys at the same time as the girls felt a rush of excitement. Now the wait for the answer. Jen turned to Amy and said, "Well Amy what do you think? Are we going to be free this weekend?"

"I don't know. We've got that big project coming up in Science and we should get to work on that."

"Yeah but it would be kind of fun to go to a movie," Jenny replied.

Trevor and Al could tell by the look on the girls faces that they were just playing around. They both had their hands deep into their coat pockets. Undoubtedly, there was a little bit of perspiration going on there.

Finally the girls turned and said, "Of course we'll go. Are you crazy? We've been waiting forever for you guys to ask us out."

"Cool. We'll meet you at the theater at about one on Saturday, O.K.?"

And with that, the plans had been set in motion. The remainder of recess was spent telling what seemed to be like every single person in the school what their discussion with Amy and Jen had been about. School was a breeze after recess, but the hard part still laid ahead of them. What were they going to do about Mr. Pilot?

Chapter 8

How to Get your Dad to Agree to Anything

That afternoon, the boys kept dreading the moment they had to face Mr. Pilot. What was he going to say about this scheme of theirs? How would he react? They really didn't know. They both hoped that he would agree. Otherwise, Al would never be able to concentrate on hockey, plus the girls would be rather upset. To kill time, they sat around and played a few Nintendo games and munched on some stale Doritos.

Al's dad finally got home at about 5:30 P.M. The two were right in the middle of a crucial combat scene when Mr. Pilot walked by and said, "Hey guys, what are you two up to?"

They both fumbled with their game gear and managed to stammer back, "Uh, nothing. Just playin some video games."

Mr. Pilot seemed to be satisfied with that answer because he just kept on heading for his room to change. Al quickly realized this might be THE perfect time to spring their wonder plan on him, so he said, "Hey dad, can I, I mean, can we talk to you for a second?"

"Sure." Mr. Pilot came back in the room and took a seat on the couch behind the two boys on the floor. "So what's on your mind?"

Trevor knowing that he was the key player in this whole plan started it off with, "Well, Mr. P, it's like this. You see, there are these two girls at school and…"

"Uh-oh, I hope we don't have to go over this whole girl issue again," Mr. Pilot stated with a gruff voice and gave his son a sideways glance that didn't show much promise.

"Wait dad, just listen to what Trevor has to say, O.K.?" pleaded Al.

"Anyway, Mr. P, these girls have been after us for I don't know how long, and you know how Al and I just try to focus on hockey, right? Well, we haven't really paid much attention to the whole thing. We just worry about skating. But, today they actually asked us out on a date! We didn't know what to do. We were being watched by the entire school, and we really didn't want to be thought of as wimps, so…"

"You said yes." Mr. Pilot was stating what Trevor was obviously going to say next.

The plan was working. Revising the info about who actually asked who out was the icing on the cake. It was a perfect way to make it seem all right to go on a date. Trevor and Al looked at each other with a huge grin and said in unison, "Yeeeeaaaaah!"

"You're the first person we've had a chance to run it by," said Al. "If you don't mind us going to a movie with Amy and Jen, we were going to go over to Trev's house for dinner and ask his mom and dad if it was O.K. with them?"

Mr. Pilot thought for what seemed like an eternity. Finally he let out a long sigh, "Oh I guess it's all right. I still don't like the idea of 5th graders going on dates, but I suppose times have changed a little since I was a youngster?"

"Thank God," Trevor thought to himself.

"Well, if that's it, I think I'm going to change. You guys better head over to Trevor's house because Mr. Eubanks might not be as accommodating as "Yours Truly"." With that, he got up from the couch and headed towards the bedroom. When they thought the coast was clear, Trevor and Al gave each other a huge high five.

"Oh man, I was soooo worried he was going to say No Way Jose," sighed Al.

"I can't believe this actually worked," Trevor said with a look of relief all over his face.

"I almost lost it when he was talking about your dad. Your dad's going to be a piece of cake compared to this!" They both laughed at Al's comments.

"C'mon, let's get going. I don't want to miss any of my mom's food," Trevor said as the two gave each other another high five.

As expected, the Eubanks were a much softer sell than Mr. Pilot. Both Trevor's mom and dad thought that it was a harmless idea. Mr. Eubanks was astounded that they were able to convince Al's father so easily. He kept saying, "I can't believe that you two talked Mr. Pilot into going along with this!" Trevor's mom kept on saying how "cute" she thought the whole thing was. That made Trev and Al kind of sick, but they really did not care, because deep down they knew their secret plan had worked! Now all that was left was to actually go on the date.

Chapter 9

The Granby

The Granby is a very old theater right in downtown Laketon. The new theater, which has 12 screens, is in the mall on the outskirts of town. Most of the kids at school went to the big theater because all of the cool movies showed there first. After all, the Granby only had two theaters, and one was really small. All four decided they would rather go to the Granby because of the huge theater with the balcony. It was a perfect place for a first date. It was quiet, and there probably would not be many kids from school there that might be inclined to bother them.

Trevor and Al got to the theater about 45 minutes early. They wanted to make sure they were the first to get there so that they could buy the tickets. Because they were so early they decided to play a few video games.

"Mortal Kombat, ooh come on Al let's play," Trev said excitedly.

"I'm sick of that game man, let's play this one," Al returned pointing to a game neither had seen before.

"The Toad's Larynx?" inquired Trevor. "This sounds like one of those weird adventure games."

"No, it's super cool. Nate was telling me all about it last week. He said that the main guy is this warped alien type guy who you control and try to blast your way into the evil army's headquarters. C'mon you've got to give it a shot!"

"O.K. just chill. I'll play, but just once."

Al was a little more interested in the whole video game scene than Trevor was. He subscribed to every game magazine so he could learn all of the secret strategies on how to win. Trevor liked to play as well, but he didn't waste his money on anything but hockey gear and hockey cards. To date his collection was nearly 2,000 cards. Once they began playing the game, it didn't take long for them to become completely engrossed.

Amy and Jen showed up about 20 minutes later. It didn't take but 30 seconds for the game to end after they showed up. Al turned around and saw Jenny for the first time. She was wearing a brand new pair of bib overalls with a flannel shirt. "Wow, you look great!"

"Thanks Al, so what time should we go in?" she replied.

"Let's go right now."

Everyone agreed they should sit up in the balcony. When they got to their seats, Trevor and Al started to sit next to each other until they realized they weren't going to the movies just by themselves this time. They quickly rearranged and sat boy-girl-boy-girl. Al, being eager to please, asked the girls if they would like any "refreshments." They both said yes, so the boys were up and out of there seats about two minutes after sitting down.

On the way to the counter, Al started poking Trev. "Can you believe it? We're actually here. I can't believe it!"

"Calm down. The movie hasn't even started yet."

"I know, I know. I'm just so excited," replied Al slightly out of breath.

"Really, I couldn't tell." The sarcasm was apparent.

Al punched Trevor in the arm as the two jumped into the concession stand line. They both got a MOVIE size popcorn which was so big, they almost needed a forklift to carry the dumb thing. The pop was almost as big. Both were definitely better suited for two people instead of one.

Luckily they got back to their seats just in time for the previews. That was always the best part of going to a movie, just seeing all the cool stuff that was about to be released. Plus the movie they were seeing today probably wasn't going to be the world's greatest. It was called *The Super Sludge,* and was based on a comic book from the 50's. Usually these movies ended up being kind of silly, but they really weren't interested in the movie that much anyway. They were there for the date.

During the previews, Trevor saw two movies that he thought would be awesome. One was a John Rover movie called The Future is Now. His movies were always jam packed with adventure and most of all-explosions. Furthermore, Trevor loved to watch martial arts movies, and John Rover always liked to play the tough karate dude. The other movie was called The Outer World which was a futuristic sci-fi thriller. After the previews, the four crouched down in their seats and got ready for the movie.

About thirty minutes into the movie, Trevor kind of nudged forward to see what was going on with Al and Jen. He noticed that both had their hands in the big popcorn bucket at the same time. "Nothin like holding hands in a vat of grease," thought Trevor to himself. Even though he was excited to be at the movies with Amy, he didn't feel comfortable in getting too touchy feely. He had noticed Amy moving closer to him on a couple of occasions,but didn't pay it much attention. Little did he know what was in store for him.

Trevor kept getting more and more involved in the movie. The special effects weren't as basic as he thought they would be, so his interest level was definitely at a high point. He had even somewhat forgotten about the people sitting around him. He happened to be still holding the huge soft drink he had bought at the concession stands. Al noticed that Trev was really focused on the movie, so he decided to play a practical joke on him. He quietly licked his left index finger and slid his hand behind Jen's back and deftly stuck it into Trevor's ear.

"AAAAAAAhhhhhhh!"

Trevor was freaked out. In an instant his soft drink went flying in the air, and everyone in the theater turned to look at him. The drink appeared to hover about three feet above their heads and then came crashing down on top of Amy. She was covered head to toe in a sticky mess of Mr. Pibb.

"Oh my god, look what you've done!" she shrieked.

"I'm sooooo sorrrrry Amy, but it wasn't my fault, really," Trevor pleaded.

"Well I've got to get some of this washed out of my clothes. My mother is going to kill me!" With that, she lurched out of her seat and headed down the aisle.

Trevor immediately turned and glared at Al. "YOU are going to die," he said with his teeth tightly clenched together.

Of course Al thought this was the funniest thing he had ever witnessed. He could barely contain his laughter. They never did get to see the end of the movie, as Amy demanded to go home. After she left, Trevor got Al in a head lock and began to give him noogies all over the place. "You deserve way worse than this, you dork!"

Apparently it didn't hurt Al that much because he just kept on laughing. In fact, he couldn't get that stupid grin off of his face all the way home!

Chapter 10

The Season Continues

The Granby incident pretty much took care of Amy. She wouldn't even look at Trevor the next week. He felt really sorry for what had happened, but he wasn't about to go apologizing for something that wasn't even his fault. So he decided to let Amy be mad and to go back to worrying about hockey. The season was coming to a close anyway. The Bobcats had only seven games remaining on their schedule. Their unblemished streak made their record 26-0! Everything seemed to be clicking for their team. The defense was strong, the goal tending was much improved, and, of course, the offense was as potent as ever. All they needed was to keep up the intensity, and everyone knew they could go all the way.

After the movie episode, Al and Trevor were not exactly on the best of terms. Embarrassing was the only way to describe the event, and Trevor was definitely going to make Al remember that he owed him, Big Time! Instead of hockey, Al directed all of his energy towards Jen. The two were constantly on the phone with each other. At school, all they did was talk to each other, sit by each other at lunch, and even stand together during recess. It was enough to make any sensible person sick to their stomach.

Power Play

The next Saturday the Bobcats had a double header. In baseball, double headers are great because you don't have to run all that much and you are outside enjoying the weather. Hockey, on the other hand, is NOT a sport that goes well with back-to-back games. It's hard enough to finish just one game, let alone TWO in a row. They usually only had two double headers a year, just for that reason. At the end of the year, playing on short rest was good practice which is why the coach arranged for this particular double header. Luckily, the team they were facing wasn't all that tough.

Coach gathered all of the players around just before the opening face-off and said,"O.K. guys today's going to be a tough day. We're going to see how ready you are for the tournament. Now, the first line will not be skating as much as usual during the first game. I need you guys fresh for the second game. So don't get down and start pouting just because you're spending more time on the pine. You'll get your chances later, O.K.? Besides, we need to give everyone some quality minutes. Let's get out there and skate hard!" With that the team formed a huddle around the coach and shouted "HUSTLE!"

The first period started well for Laketon. They had many power play chances and scored on their first two tries. Trevor added a break away goal late in the period to make the score 3-0. The team appeared to be rolling along. Everyone except Al that is. He was lethargic and unmotivated. If there was a loose puck, he wouldn't even try to retrieve it. To the crowd, it was apparent that he was completely out of sync.

On the way to the locker room, Trevor noticed that Amy and Jen were in the stands. Al obviously knew they were coming because he motioned them to come down by the walkway to talk to them before going into the locker room. Trevor was skating behind Al, so when he got to the walkway, Al was already waiting for him. "Trev, man, I'm really sorry about the Granby. I told Amy all about it, and she's cool with it now. She wants to talk to you, so just wait here until they get here o.k.?"

"Al, this isn't the time or the place; we're in the middle of a hockey game!"

"Oh yeah, these guys are really tough," Al responded in a sarcastic tone.

"I'm not interested right now. Maybe after the second game," replied Trevor as he walked toward the locker room shaking his head. Al stayed behind to chat with the girls. When he finished, he too headed to the locker room.

By the time he arrived in the locker room, the coach had already begun his intermission speech. As Al walked in, coach paused and looked scornfully at Al and said, "So good of you to join your teammates, Al." The locker room was silent as Al took his spot on a nearby bench with a smirk on his face. The coach finished his speech and told the rest of the team how well they were skating. By then, it was time to get back on the ice and warm up before the second period. The team stood up and began to head back to the rink when the coach said loudly in his typically booming voice, "Al, can I see you for a sec before you head out?"

All eyes turned to the pair as they began a little chat in the far corner of the locker room. "Where's your mind son? You're just not here today. You skated timidly the first period, and then you can't make it in here for the strategy talk? I don't understand what's going on."

Al shuffled his feet with his head hung low. "I don't know coach. I'm sorry I was late; it won't happen again."

"Well, I think you need some time to think about your actions. You'll be on the bench for the second period."

"But..."

"NO buts about it. Now get back out there, and show me you're ready to skate!"

Al turned dejectedly toward the door and walked back to the rink. What was his father going to say now? He had never been benched before, for any reason. A huge knot began to develop in his stomach and throat. He thought to himself, "Why did I have to go talk to those girls?"

But he knew they weren't the real problem. The real problem was that hockey just wasn't as important to him anymore. There were other things that were just as important-like girls, having fun, and going to the movies. It was just so hard because he knew his dad would be disappointed. Ever since he was a Mighty Mite, his dad had constantly pushed him. By now, it had finally caught up to him. As the second period started, there was Al sitting on the bench right next to the coach with a tear in his eye. Up in the stands his father started wondering why his boy wasn't out on the ice. Confrontation was inevitable, and Al had a feeling he was going to be in trouble. Big trouble.

Chapter 11

Consequences

The Bobcats continued to play tough hockey throughout the second period. Trevor was his usual amazing self, assisting on two goals and scoring two of his own. The only mistake came when Toby tried to clear the puck out, and one of the opposing skaters intercepted the pass and had a wide open shot on goal. With that, the score at the second intermission was 7-1. The first game of the double header was over for all practical purposes. Al had remained on the bench the entire period without so much as muttering a word. The tears faded away, but the knot in his stomach was stronger than ever.

Mr. Pilot was ready and waiting for both the coach and his son by the walkway to the locker room. Needless to say, he wanted to know why his son was not on the ice the second period. Holding back his anger, he pulled the coach aside. "Can you please tell me why my boy wasn't out on the ice the last period?" he said with clenched teeth.

"Mr. Pilot, no need to get angry. I was just letting him sit and think about whether or not he wanted to skate. You saw the first period. Al was not his usual self. He seemed distracted. And during the intermission, he didn't make it into the locker room until I was halfway done with my strategy talk. And, to be honest, this isn't the first incident."

"Oh, I see," Mr. Pilot responded with a sigh. "Do you mind if I have a talk with my son?"

"No, go right ahead."

Al had spotted his father standing by the walkway, so he was lingering around the edge of the ice waiting to be called over. He knew that going into the locker room was not the right idea. His dad would more than likely barge in and yank him out in front of everyone. It was better this way. When he saw his coach head toward the locker room, he knew it was his turn.

"Can you tell me what in God's name is going on?" Mr. Pilot barked.

"Coach is upset with my attitude, I guess," replied Al in a barely audible tone.

"He told me you've been a little late for the team meetings, and not just today."

"I have a lot of stuff going on, Dad," Al pleaded.

"No excuse. Could one of those reasons be someone named Jen? I saw you two talking during the last intermission. Is that why you were late?"

"No…"

"I don't buy it Al. Your team is in the middle of a great season, and you risk that by not giving hockey 100%! Do you know how that makes me feel?" Al hung his head and stared at his skates. A tear welled up and fell directly onto his laces. "You and I are going home now. We're going to have a serious talk, and then we're going to make some time for a little extra practice down at the pond. Do you understand?"

"But I can't leave dad. We've got another game!" By now Al was sobbing, making it difficult for him to even breath.

"That's too bad. Plus, I don't think they need your services against this team. Now I want you to go into that locker room and tell the coach exactly what I just said. Go on!"

Al slowly walked to the locker room. Inside things were pretty quiet. The coach didn't have much to say, so he just let his team rest up a little.

Al headed toward the coach, who was taping one of the player's stick. As he approached, the coach looked up and saw the expression on Al's face. "What's wrong son?"

"Uhhh, coach…ummmm…I'm not…(long sigh) going….to be able(gulp)…to ahhh skate…anymore…today. My dad wants to…," he managed to spit out.

"O.K., O.K. I understand. Al, I want you to think about your actions today and be back here on Tuesday for practice. O.K.?"

Al nodded his head and left the locker room under the stares of his fellow teammates. "Think about my actions" Al thought to himself. "Like I wanted any of this to happen!"

The ride home was done in complete silence. Mr. Pilot stared straight ahead, and Al sat looking out the window slumped into the passenger seat. When they got home, all that Mr. Pilot said was, "Wait here until I get my gear." After about ten minutes, Al's father returned dressed in his skating gear. "C'mon. We're going to the pond. Grab a shovel."

During the walk to the pond, Mr. Pilot started his speech. "Al, you have so much talent for the sport of hockey. Your skills could take you a long way. But all I ever see is you wasting your time and talents. You need to have your heart and soul into this sport. Otherwise, you just become another nameless face. Do you understand me?" Al just nodded his head in false agreement.

"All I ever try to do is instill a good work ethic that will enable you to succeed. That's half the battle right there. I've seen plenty of fancy skaters who never make it because they refuse to put in the time it takes to be a good hockey player at the next level. That is NOT going to happen to you!"

Al cleared the rink as his dad sat and watched. There was about four new inches of snow on the ice from the last storm, so it was not easy to shovel. After thirty minutes, Al had cleared off enough space so they could practice. This was not an uncommon event. Mr. Pilot had taken Al here many times over the course of his young life. Sometimes it was to help and sometimes it was to watch. Most often, it was to practice which was never much fun. Al often remembered when his dad taught him how to skate when he was two. He had just learned how to walk nine months prior to his first skating lessons. Those were much happier times with his father. There was no pressure to succeed. There was only him, his father, and a fold up chair to help balance the small skater. Right now, he wished those days could be rekindled, but he knew the truth would not allow that.

For the next three and half hours, Mr. Pilot took his son through countless stick handling, puck handling, and skating drills. Not doing it correctly the first time meant he would have to do it another ten times. The last drill was sprints around the perimeter of the skating area. The first time around it took Al ten seconds.

"Ten! We're not leaving until you get that time down to eight!" shouted Mr. Pilot.

The next time around, "NINE POINT FIVE! BETTER!"

This routine went on until the eleventh time around the ice when Al finally broke that eight second barrier. "All right son! Way to go! I'm proud of you!" Mr. Pilot barked with joy. Al wasn't interested, however. All he wanted to do was go home, eat supper, take a bath, and go to bed- which is exactly what he did. When his father came in to his room to talk, he was already sound asleep. Mr. Pilot bent over, pulled the covers up, patted Al on the head, and quietly left the room.

Chapter 12

Fatigue Sets In

On Sunday, Al did not wake up until 11:00. When he saw what time it was, he jumped out of bed and raced downstairs. There was no one in the house. "MOM, DAD?" he shouted. No answer. "Where could everyone be?" he thought to himself. He searched and searched throughout the house. Finally, he went into the kitchen. On the table there was a note which read:

Al,
    We all went to church this morning but thought you could use the rest, so we let you sleep in a little bit longer. We will be back around noon to have a nice lunch. Oh, your dad would like to go down to the pond later with you too.

Love Mom and Dad
P.S. Wake up you lughead! Theresa

"I can't believe he wants to practice today too," Al muttered to himself. Couldn't he see how tired he was. He had slept for over 13 hours!

After he read the note, Al poured himself a bowl of Chocolate Crunch Berries and went into the family room to watch some television. Before he could get situated in the "comfy" chair, the phone rang. "Oh Great!"

On the fourth ring he finally picked up the receiver. "Hello, Pilot residence."

"Hey stupid, I thought you were never going to answer."

"Oh, Hi Trev."

"What happened yesterday, man?" inquired Trevor.

"My dad kind of flipped, if you know what I mean. How'd the other game go?"

"We won 5-2, but it wasn't as close as the score was. So, what did you guys do for the rest of the day? I wanted to come over but my dad wouldn't let me. He said you guys needed some time alone."

Al told Trevor all about their fun practice session. The two jabbered away for what might have been forty minutes. During that time, Al had managed to deftly finish his bowl of cereal. Coordination was definitely NOT a problem when food was involved.

"Yeah, can you believe it? He wants to practice again today!"

"Do you want me to show up at the pond? It might help mellow him out," offered Trevor.

"I guess so. I don't know. You decide, o.k.? I think we'll probably be there around two thirty or three."

The two were still on the phone when Al's family came home from church.

"Uh listen, my parents just showed up. I gotta go. Yeah, see ya." Al hung the phone up and stood to see how church went. Maybe if he was extra nice, his dad would forget all about their scheduled practice session.

Al greeted them in the kitchen and everything seemed to be back to normal. Well, at least semi-normal. His mom and sister started preparing lunch as he set the table, and his dad was off watching something on t.v. already. It was probably some kind of sporting event. All his dad ever watched was either sports or some kind of nature show. Al and Theresa had to plead with him every Thursday so they could watch their favorite t.v. shows.

Lunch went smoothly enough. The chicken sandwiches were terrific, and the conversation never turned to hockey, which was always a plus. As Al started to clear the table, Mr. Pilot said, "Well, we should probable give our stomach some rest before we hit the ice, right Al?"

"Oh, you still want to go today?" replied Al with a glimmer of hope in his voice.

"You bet. Yesterday was ground breaking. Or should I say ice breaking." Mr. Pilot chuckled to himself. "I think that with a few more sessions like that, we'll have ourselves a hockey star."

"What time did you want to go out dad?" A hint of dejection could be sensed in Al's voice.

"Oh, I don't know. Let's see how we feel in an hour." Mr. Pilot got out of his seat and headed towards the basement for some relaxation.

"What's the matter hon?" Mrs. Pilot asked her son, who was visibly upset.

"I don't really want to practice today."

"Well, I'm sure your father won't be quite as hard on you today. I know he can be tough on you, but he's only trying to help, you know."

Al thought to himself, "Yeah I KNOW. I live through it every day Mom."

His mom was always supportive of both her children. Sometimes, though, Al felt like she really didn't know what was going on with him. Couldn't she see how much pressure was on him to succeed? But it wasn't her fault. It was his father's. Al dreamed of the day he wouldn't have to do everything just to please his father. The real question was whether or not that day would ever come?

Like clockwork, the Pilot's were on the ice at two thirty that Sunday. Maybe his mom was right. Today's practice session wasn't nearly as tough as yesterday's. Mr. Pilot and Al skated back and forth trying fancy passes and new skating moves together.

"Hey Mr. P! How's it goin?" Trevor shouted as he approached the pond.

Power Play

On the ice, the two stopped and skated over to where Trevor was standing. "Well, hi there Trev. Did you want to skate with us for a bit?"

"Sure. It's such a nice day!" The weather had definitely turned for the better this past week. Instead of the bitter Arctic winds that Minnesota was famous for, a warm breeze from the south had brought mild temperatures. March in Minnesota meant one thing, and one thing only; Winter was about to end for another year. This old pond would soon be buzzing with wildlife once again.

The rest of the afternoon was spent playing two-on-one with Mr. Pilot. Both Trevor and Al had a ton of fun. No one kept score. It was just a great day to be outside enjoying the weather and the game.

When it was over, Al went to Trevor's house to check out his NHL'96 video game. On the way over, Trevor asked Al, "That wasn't bad today. Was he tougher on you yesterday?"

"Try two hundred percent tougher! He's never as intense when you're around. Then he's trying to be the cool dad, you know?"

"Yeah, I guess. You've just got to learn to ignore him sometimes. Relax. Have fun."

Trevor didn't realize that was exactly what Al would like to do, but the chances of that happening weren't exactly high. The remainder of the day was spent pretending to be pro hockey players while playing Trev's new video game. Aside from this brief reprieve, the practices with his father continued over the next few weeks. Sometimes Al would practice for nearly four hours a day. This insane ritual had sapped Al of any spare energy. His dad figured that was the best way to get him to focus on hockey rather than the girl situation.

Chapter 13

As The Season Winds Down

The Bobcats had continued their winning ways all year long. With two games left in the regular season, they had managed to post a record of 30-0 and a #1 ranking in the state polls. One game was against Crookston, which was always a tough team, and the other was the season finale at Riverplace. Everyone was starting to get pumped up for what was going to be the game of the year. Riverplace also had an impressive year following their loss to the Bobcats early in the season. Both teams would be geared up for the match the following week. First the Bobcats needed to get past a pesky Crookston team.

    Al and his father had practiced on the pond every night since the double header. Al was getting completely burned out by the constant wear and tear. Not only did he have to work hard during the regular team practice, but he had to do even more for his father. Tired was the only word to describe Al's physical state. Today was worse than any of the days before. The fatigue had definitely set into his legs.

    The first period started with Laketon on their heels. The Cougars of Crookston had come prepared to play today. They immediately took the opening face-off from Trevor and put pressure on the Bobcat defense. Four minutes into the game, with some quick passing and superb teamwork, the Cougars found themselves in front one-zip.

"C'mon guys, hustle!" shouted Al's coach.

The pressure did not stop. Laketon struggled just to get the puck over the center line. Their break came when Zach Punch, who skated on the third line, stole an errant pass and swiftly moved into Cougar territory. With a double fake to the right side, he slid the puck under the goalie's outstretched glove to tie the game at one.

During the intermission after the first period, the Bobcats all sat quietly listening to the specific plan of attack laid out by their coach. Their pressure offense would be in place led by Trevor, Al, and Kevin. Coverage on defense was changed to ensure that there were at least two back to help on a possible breakaway. During this time, Al sat with his head in between his knees. He was not feeling well at all. At first he shrugged it off as not having a good breakfast, but he really felt like he needed to vomit. Just before they went back out on the ice, he snuck into the bathroom and did just that.

The second period started out much better for Laketon. The new offense threw the Cougars for a loop. Trevor scored two quick goals to give them a three to one lead. The opposing team quickly called a timeout to stop the momentum. During the timeout, Al clung to the sideboards. When time was called, he went up to the coach and asked, "Coach, can I sit out for a few minutes? I don't feel so hot."

"Not now Al; we've really got to put some pressure on them now!" Coach patted him on the helmet as Al pushed off the sideboard.

As Al began to skate to his left wing position, he began to feel really dizzy. For the next three minutes of the game he did nothing but skate slowly in his assigned area. When it was time for his shift to be over, he was glad to have a chance to rest.

"What kind of skating was that?!" shouted his coach, as he took a spot at the end of the bench. "You weren't doing anything out there.

Don't you want to put these guys away?" His coach crouched down and looked at Al solemnly. "I'm putting you on the next line in place of Zach. You can pull a double shift." The coach stood quickly and regained his focus on the game.

Al couldn't do it. He simply could not skate anymore. He was too tired. He felt the queasiness coming over him again. He went to the corner of the bench and vomited one more time, this time in the trash can. After he was done, he took his seat. Just as he was about to sit down the coach yelled, "LINE SHIFT, C'MON GUYS. LET'S GO!!"

Al rarely skated with the third line, so he didn't really know his role. Should he try to be the leader or should he just sit back and let the others perform? He decided the only way to get the coach off of his back was to try and skate as hard as possible. Before they jumped on the ice, Laketon had dumped the puck into Cougar territory. Crookston was a little slow getting the puck out of the corner. Al pushed off the bench and started to skate hard to the corner. Just as he crossed the blue line, number 15 of the Cougars flicked the puck weakly to one of his teammates. Al raced in and knocked the puck down out of midair. In a flash he was alone against the opposing goalie. With his wrists cocked, he let go with a powerful shot. The goalie slid to his left trying to block the puck. He was just a fraction of a second late as the puck ricocheted off of his pad and into the net. 4-1!

His teammates came crashing in on him as he raised his stick weakly to signal a goal. With a barrage of pats and "Way to go's," he skated toward the bench. The coach was there to greet him. "Nice job, Al. Now let's do it again!"

Al could not believe his ears. The coach was making him stay on the ice. It was probably some kind of punishment for the past few weeks. That last goal had zapped him of any energy he had left. Doggedly, he skated to center ice for the face-off. For the next two minutes, he hung pretty tough, but then the dizziness came rushing back. At first he tried to shake it off, but with no success. Soon he was seeing double images of everyone on the ice. It was almost as if he was in some kind of dream state. Everything around him seemed to be completely unreal. The sounds from the crowd came crashing down on him. "SKATE AL, SKATE AL!" he heard, or at least thought he heard, from somewhere near the bench. So with his remaining strength, he pushed off and started heading toward the goal…except it was the wrong goal. He had managed to pick up some speed at the blue line but then started to wobble. As he approached Toby, he slipped and fell, sliding head first into the goal post with a loud "CLANGGG!"

The referee blew his whistle and skated towards the hump of mass on the ice. Al's coach, knowing that he was hurt, scrambled onto the ice from his spot on the bench. His father was already on his way down the stands. Trevor was the first to get to Al besides Toby. "Al, how are you? Al?"

There was no answer. Trevor carefully shook him trying to get him to react. Nothing. Quickly he jumped to his feet and shouted, "Somebody get a doctor! He's hurt bad!"

Of course, the paramedics were already rushing onto the ice to see what was wrong. Fortunately, there was a paramedic crew at every game. By now there was a swarm of people standing around Al as he lay on the ice face down. His helmet was cracked right down the middle. Still there was no reaction from Al. His father kept muttering, "Oh my god, Oh my god." With extreme caution, the paramedics were able to turn Al over and onto a stretcher. After that they carried him to an awaiting ambulance. On the walk to the ambulance, Jeff Pilot clutched his son's lifeless hand hoping there would be some sign of life.

Chapter 14

The Fog Sets In

When Al woke up, he didn't have on any of his hockey equipment, and he was lying in a strange bed. Focusing his eyes was a difficult chore at first. It felt as though he was in a deep fog or haze. After a few minutes, his eyes finally adjusted the bright lights. Surrounding him were both of his parents, Trevor, and a couple of other people in white coats. It was then that he figured out where he was-in a hospital.

One of the doctors spoke quietly and reassuringly to him. "Al, I'm Dr. Booker. You've had an accident. You have a severe concussion. Do you remember hitting the pole?"

"Nnno, not really," he managed to mutter. Speaking was a difficult chore, as his mouth felt as dry as the Kalahari desert.

"Well, you'll need to rest here for a couple of days so that we can run some tests on you to make sure that you are all right, o.k.?"

"Yeah, sure, I guess. Can I get something to drink please?" With that response, the doctors left and a nurse returned to give him some water.

"Son, how are you feeling?" asked Al's dad.

"Pretty groggy right now. I really feel like just sleeping."

"That's the one thing you can't do," replied his mother. "We've been waiting here for over an hour to see you wake up. When you've had a concussion as severe as yours, you need to stay awake for at least 12 hours. It's possible that if you sleep your brain might just shut down. Do you understand?"

"No, not really."

"Well, we'll stay here and keep you company for a while. You just relax and try not to over-exert yourself."

"Where was she when I was over-exerting myself on the pond for the past week and half?" Al thought to himself.

His parents and Trevor stayed with him most of the night. Whenever he was about to fall asleep Trevor would make some silly comment to keep him awake. During those long hours, Al's head started to pound. He had never had a headache even close to matching this one. Trevor's parents picked him up around midnight so he could get some rest. Before he left, he promised Al he would be back first thing in the morning.

At about three in the morning, the doctors came back in to check on Al's condition. They did a few routine tests to make sure it was safe for him to sleep. After the tests turned out positive, the doctor turned to Al's parents and said, "I think we should all let Al sleep for a little while. We will be constantly monitoring him throughout the night to make sure he's stabilizing." After she had discussed Al's condition with them, she motioned them to the door. Al really liked how the doctor treated him. She acted like he was a real person and not just some stupid kid.

As the group walked outside and shut the door, Dr. Booker asked to talk to the Pilots in private. They agreed and headed to a small office tucked away in the corner of the hospital.

"Come in, have a seat," offered Dr. Booker.

"So, is he going to be O.K.?" asked Mr. Pilot.

"Well, that's why I wanted to have a little chat with you. Your son's head injury was not our main worry, Mr. and Mrs. Pilot."

"What do you mean it wasn't your main worry?" inquired Mr. Pilot suspiciously.

"We think your son is going to be fine. However, the reason he didn't respond as quickly as we would have liked is because his body was going through extreme dehydration. His blood tests showed his body's fluid level to be at a dangerously low level. As his doctor, I need to know why he was in this kind of condition. Obviously, Al is a hockey player. Has he been practicing a lot lately?"

Mr. Pilot shifted uncomfortably in his seat. "He plays on the best Squirt team in the state. They're having a terrific season, and lately I've been, uh, working with him a little extra. But I don't think that would be the cause of this, do you honey?"

"Oh come on, Jeff. You've been drilling that boy for the last two weeks. He barely has enough strength to eat when you come home from that stupid pond," replied Mrs. Pilot agitatedly.

"But I'm just trying to do what's best for the boy. He has the talent to really make something of himself. He can make it."

"Mr. Pilot," began Dr. Booker in a very soft and soothing voice, "You're son is eleven years old. Intense physical activity like that is going to lead to this kind of dehydration. His body is just too young to handle that kind of strain. You must be very careful, especially now, because Al is not going to have very much energy for a while. His system needs some down time to regain some of his strength. All that I'm asking is that you take it easy on him for the time being. I will be monitoring Al tomorrow, so hopefully he can go home soon. I hope you see where I am coming from."

Mr. Pilot nodded slowly. "Yes, I appreciate all that you've done for our son. We will have to work on some things. Thank you." The three stood and shook one another's hands.

On their walk to the waiting room, Mr. Pilot kept shaking his head. He couldn't believe this was happening to his son. The Pilot's sat in silence in the waiting room for nearly thirty minutes. Finally Mr. Pilot spoke. "Jo Beth, do you think I was pushing him too hard?"

Mrs. Pilot leaned over to him and gently stroked his hand. "Honey, you've been hard on Al for a long time. You want him to succeed so badly that you end up pushing him too hard. He's just a boy. He likes to play video games and go to the movies. He's not a professional hockey player, and he might never be one. Could you just relax a little bit around him? He loves hockey, and if it's something that he'll continue to be interested in, great. But let him make some of the choices for a change."

Mr. Pilot slumped into his chair. No one had ever told him that before, but it was something that needed to be said. This whole incident was beginning to make him realize the kind of pressure he had been putting on his son. As he sat there, all he could think about were the countless practice sessions and the seemingly endless pep talks he had given Al over the course of his life. "It's amazing he still wants to play hockey!" he thought to himself. After hours of contemplation, Jeff Pilot came to the realization that he would need to make some changes in how he dealt with his son. In the morning, he would definitely have to have a talk with Al.

Chapter 15

Tasteless

The following day Al had the dubious honor of tasting hospital food for the first time. Was it the fact that he had been groggy or was the food just plain awful? No matter how hard he tried, he could not taste the food that had been put in front of him. It looked decent enough: scrambled eggs, toast, mashed potatoes, and juice, but looks can sometimes be deceiving. He was munching on a piece of tasteless toast when his parents walked into the room.

"Hi hon, how're ya feeling today?" beamed his mother. He must have looked a little better because she was smiling from ear to ear.

"I feel a lot better. A little tired though, I guess."

"How's the food?" asked his dad.

"I'll let you know when I can actually taste it," Al quickly replied.

The three of them all shared a good laugh over that one. His parents had just eaten breakfast, so they were well aware of the culinary skills of the Laketon Hospital chefs. They chatted for awhile until Mr. Pilot looked at his wife and asked, "Say Jo Beth, do you think you could leave your two boys alone for a minute? I've got some stuff to talk about with Al."

Without a word, Al's mother left the room. A strange and awkward silence fell over the room. Mr. Pilot was fidgety and nervous. It took a few minutes before he regained enough composure to start the discussion.

"Son, your doctor, Mrs. Booker…" he started.

"Yeah, isn't she great. She's been so nice."

"I know. But that's not really what I want to talk about," Mr. Pilot said as he stared out the window overlooking the semi-frozen lake that seemingly stretched for miles. Al couldn't figure out what was going on with his dad. He sat in his bed with a quizzical look as if trying to understand what was happening. He had never seen his father like this before. "Well, uh, Dr. Booker had a little chat with your mother and I last night after you had fallen asleep."

"Yeah, what did she say?"

"She was worried about you, son. You see, your head injury was pretty bad, but you should have regained consciousness sooner than you did."

"Is something wrong with me, dad? Am I going to die?" Al asked worriedly.

Mr. Pilot patted Al's arm reassuringly. "No, no nothing like that. She said that the reason you took so long to come to was because your body was severely dehydrated. Your body was literally starving for water. She wanted to know how that was possible for such a young boy, so we told her about all of our extra practice sessions lately."

"I'm sure that wasn't it, dad. The whole team has been under a lot of pressure to stay undefeated you know and…" Al was cut off before he could finish his sentence.

"Then why isn't the whole team in the hospital today?" Mr. Pilot shot back and then looked down at his shoes. "I guess what I'm trying to say is that I'm really sorry for putting you through that kind of torture. I did some serious thinking and had a long talk with your mother last night about you. I've always wanted the best for you, but sometimes I get too pushy in trying to make you the best hockey player in the world.

You know it was my dream to go professional, but I never got the chance. I just wanted to make sure that you had the chance. I never took the time to see if that's what you wanted, and for that, I'm sorry." A few tears were beginning to well in both of their eyes.

"Dad?"

"What son?"

"I do want to play hockey. I just don't want to be so serious about it. At least not now. Who knows what will happen in the future. Maybe I will turn pro." There was a long pause before Al finished, "And maybe I won't. I just don't know. That's way too far in the future."

"Things are definitely going to change Al. I'm not going to put so much pressure on you anymore. It might take some time, but I think that we can change, don't you?"

"Yeah, I sure hope so." With that, the two gave each other a huge hug. For Al, it felt as though the weight of the world had been lifted off his shoulders. "This whole thing really scared me, son. I don't want it to happen again."

"Neither do I," sighed Al.

Dr. Booker arrived at that moment. "Oh, I'm sorry. It looks like you two are in the middle of something. I'll come back later."

"No, stay doc. We're done here. I want to thank you so much for talking to us last night. It really helped."

"Hey, I was just doing my job. Speaking of my job, how's the goal post warrior today?"

"I'm feeling great!"

Al's dad started for the door to get his wife when Al spoke up. "Dad, now that you're not going to be putting so much pressure on me..."

"Yes son, what can I do for you?"

"Well, can you give Theresa all of the left over pressure for awhile? I mean, at least until I regain my strength."

Mr. Pilot looked at his son and broke out into a hearty laugh.

Chapter 16

Season Finale At Riverplace

The last game of the season was usually just a tune-up for the state tournament, but not this year. Too much was at stake for both teams. Laketon was focused on finishing off their undefeated season, while Riverplace was ready to exact some revenge for a game they felt they should have won earlier in the year. Just walking into the arena made one realize this was no ordinary hockey game. There was a definite energy in the air, not only from the teams on the ice for warm ups but also from the parents and fans in the stands.

Trevor was particularly psyched for this game. He knew the importance of what they were trying to accomplish. A place in state hockey history would be a certainty if they won here today. As he skated around the rink glancing up into the stands, he couldn't remember a more enthusiastic atmosphere, not even at any of the tournament championships he had already experienced. People he had never seen at any of his other games were in the stands today. Some of his buddies from school were there, even kids he usually didn't hang around. Mr. Winslow was even there with the school's cam corder to capture this historic event on film. A local television crew had even gathered to cover the game. The stakes were definitely higher than usual.

The two teams warmed up in silence. Everyone was ready to play. Whenever they had a chance, players would glare at the opposition letting them know intimidation was not going to be a factor today. Trevor skated up to Toby who had been practicing his glove saves. "Well big guy, this is it. How do ya feel today?

"Nervous, but I'm ready," Toby replied never once looking up from his stance. Judging by his concentration, Trevor knew that Toby would not be backing down today.

The clock ticked down. Less than two minutes until the opening face-off. That was the Bobcats' signal to gather by the bench for one last pep talk. Coach was waiting for them as they skated in solemnly. "Well, gentlemen, today's the day we see what we're made of. I know that you are all anxious to get this thing going, so I'm going to be brief. If you can't get pumped up for this game, then nothing I can say will motivate you either. I just want to let you know that I am extremely proud of how you have skated this year. You have definitely come together as a team. Now let's get out there and get after 'em just like we've been doing all year long!"

"ONE, TWO, THREE..."

"HUSTLE!"

Up in the stands Al leaned over to his dad and said, "Man, I wish I could be out there today. This is what we've wanted all year."

"I know, son. You'll be back next year. We just have to cheer them on now." The doctors at the hospital urged the Pilots to keep Al from hockey for the remainder of the year. He needed time to recuperate and replenish his body's water. Al was totally against that idea, but his father insisted on making him rest. Al knew now that his dad really did want to change, which was great with him.

The referee blew his whistle, time for the game to begin. Both teams skated into their respective positions. The arena grew deafly quiet. The puck dropped. The game was on! The first five minutes began with a tough defensive battle. Neither team was able to generate any good shots on goal. Trevor and Zeke had already exchanged a few shoves here and there. A blowout didn't seem likely with the way these two teams were skating.

Riverplace looked like they were going to score first when number 12, Ryan stole the puck from Andrew and swooped in on Toby. Toby positioned himself low, knowing that Riverplace liked to keep the puck on the ice. Ryan faked to the open right side of the net. Toby slid to his left. Ryan then shot to the other side. Toby pushed his stick back to the right just in time to deflect the puck into the corner. Trevor raced to snatch up the puck. He spun to his right and noticed Zach was wide open at the red line. He immediately sent the puck in Zach's direction. It was a pinpoint pass that gave Zach a breakaway chance. In another moment the crowd was cheering wildly, the Bobcats led 1-0!

"Nice pass man!" shouted Zach as he greeted Trevor with a high five.

"Thanks! Let's keep it up!" Zach's improvement lately had made him the obvious choice as Al's replacement at right wing on the #1 line. He was going to be tough for Al to beat out next year.

Riverplace was not about to quit. They scored less than three minutes later on a power play to knot the score at one. A couple of minutes later they added another one to take the lead as the first period came to a close.

Both teams skated off towards their locker room. Al jumped to his feet and headed there too. "Where you going son?"

"I want to talk to my team."

Al waited until the coach had finished laying out the plans for the next period before he spoke. "Uh, coach, can I just say a few words?"

"Sure, Al. How are you feeling?"

"Pretty good. Uh, listen guys, you're skating pretty well but not as well as you can. Just relax out there. Let the game come to you. These guys will fold in the end. Keep up the pressure and good things will happen."

The team appeared to be motivated with Al's talk as they left the locker room for the second period. Al returned to his seat in the stands. The second period started out much better for the Bobcats. They controlled the puck entirely. Riverplace didn't even manage to cross into their zone for the first eight minutes. Laketon had numerous scoring chances but just couldn't get things going. Frustration was beginning to set in, and the expressions on the Bobcat faces told the whole story. What did they have to do to score on these guys?

With two minutes left in the period, they started to force the issue. With every chance they could get, they let go of a shot. Most weren't even close to going in, (although a few had been right on target), but the Tiger goalie was able to stop them. With the puck in the corner, Trevor skated over to try and clear to one of the defensemen. After a struggle, he was able to wrestle the puck away from Zeke and pass it back hoping to get it to either Chuckie or Steve, their two defensemen. Zeke took off after the puck. Chuckie was the first to get to the puck but couldn't handle it cleanly. Zeke came racing towards the puck, jabbed it away towards center ice, and was off on a breakaway. Steve hustled to get back but was too far behind. When Zeke crossed over their blue line he dove for his legs but missed. Zeke finished off the break with a clean shot to the upper left corner of the net that whistled by Toby. 3-1 Riverplace!

The second period buzzer sounded. Before leaving the ice, Zeke skated right up to Trevor. "I can't believe you guys are undefeated. You're nothing. You aren't even close to scoring. I don't even think I need to come back for the last period. This game is over."

Trevor's blood began to boil. "I think you might want to because if you don't, you'll miss the excitement of your team losing."

"Whatever ya wimp, you are sooo over-rated, you loser!" Zeke yelled as he headed off the ice.

Trevor did not move an inch. Instead he just stared at Zeke until he had left the ice. He then skated quickly to the side and met up with his team in the locker room. "I want you guys to look for me whenever you can. Zeke thinks that we're done, that we're just a bunch of wimps. Well, I think we can show him otherwise. We've come to far to let a chump like that beat us!"

Everyone in the locker room looked at Trevor with wide eyes. Trevor was not the team's cheerleader by any means. He usually quietly went about his business. So when he spoke like that, everyone was kind of surprised. The last time they had seen that kind of intensity was on the pond, and up in Canada, a few months back. The Bobcats returned to the ice in a subdued fashion, not knowing what was in store for them. Al met Trev on the bench. He had snuck down during the intermission so he could be with his team.

"Trev, you've got to make it happen," Al pleaded.

"Don't worry, I'm motivated now. That idiot Zeke just called me a loser. I think I need to show him who's the loser."

"Show him your moves, big guy!" Al smiled. He knew what was in store now. Whenever Trevor got mad, he skated twice as hard, which is about five times better than any Squirt in Minnesota. "C'mon Bobcats!" he shouted as the teams took the ice.

The referee dropped the puck and Trevor scooped it up and began to weave in and out of the Tiger defense like a slalom skier. He skated down the right side, then right before he got to the goal, crossed over to the left and let a backhanded shot fly. The puck hit nothing but the back of the net as the goalie was caught off guard.

Trevor skated over to Zeke and said, "That's one, you moron."

The only reply Zeke had was to say, "Shut up!"

Two minutes later Zach found Trevor across the rink and threaded a nifty pass that gave Trevor his second goal of the game. Once again Trevor found Zeke. This time he skated by and just held up two of his fingers.

Al laughed as he had watched the whole thing unravel for Riverplace. The look on Zeke's face was something he would never forget. By the end of the game, the Tigers were completely exhausted and stunned. They had never seen anything like what had happened in the third period before. The final score was 8-3 in favor of the Bobcats. Trevor finished the game with five goals and three assists. Zeke could do nothing but leave the rink quietly. The Bobcats finished the season undefeated! They now had a share of state hockey history. They were the first Squirt team to go undefeated the entire season. The only thing left for them was to win the state tournament, which was nearly a "sure thing."

"Wow! I wouldn't have believed it unless I saw it myself," stammered Mr. Pilot as he had made his way down to the bench too. "I've never seen a burst of scoring like that before!"

"I know, he's pretty amazing isn't he," replied Al.

"You're right about that. That kid is amazing! Almost magical!"

Al wanted to talk to Trevor, but he was surrounded by the t.v. crew interviewing him about his performance. He was a definite star in the making. Al would just have to wait until later when the team went out for pizza to celebrate.

Chapter 17

Celebration

The team met at Broadway Pizza at five o'clock. The restaurant was packed with people. The whole town had seemingly turned up to celebrate today's win. Al was saving a place for Trevor at one end of a long table for the team. Trevor was a little late getting there because of everyone that had wanted to talk to him. The team wore their home jerseys, since the away ones were all sweaty. Toby and Nate were over playing video games with a bunch of other guys from the team. The rest were sitting waiting for the coach to get there so they could order some pizzas. They were all HUNGRY!

Trevor finally showed up and headed towards Al. He slapped him on the back as he sat down. "How ya feeling Al?"

"Great after today. Man, you were amazing out there today!"

"Zeke kind of got on my nerves, so I felt like I had something to prove, you know?" replied Trev.

"Yeah, I think everyone saw that."

The two laughed in between the hoots and hollers of the raucous crowd, as Al told Trev about the expression on Zeke's face during the entire third period. Their coach finally showed up and gave a congratulatory speech. Even the parents were hooting and hollering. The entire restaurant was in good spirits. After the speech, they ordered nearly twenty pizzas for the team.

While they were waiting for their order, Trevor said, "We sure missed you out there today, Al. When do you think you'll be back?"

"It's funny because I guess I haven't talked to you since I returned from the hospital."

"I know. We've been so busy getting ready for the game today."

"Well, the concussion I had was only one thing that was wrong."

"What are you talkin about?" asked Trevor with a confused look on his face.

"The doctor said the real problem was that I was severely dehydrated, probably from all those extra practices with my dad."

Trevor took a sip of his Coke, "Yeah, I couldn't believe how hard he was working you."

"After the doctor explained it to my parents, they had a long talk about how hard my dad pushes me and how intense he is about hockey all the time."

"And…?"

"My dad came into my room the next day, and we had a long talk. He's going to try to loosen up and just let me play. Supposedly, no more intense pressure."

"Man, that's great, Al. It's going to make all the difference, you'll see. My dad doesn't really put any pressure on me, and I think that's helped. I mean, I don't know what I would do if I had to play under all that pressure, you know?"

"Yeah, I think it's going to be a lot better."

Just then, the pizzas arrived to shouts of cheer from the team. Immediately, they started grabbing slices of pizza so fast, almost as though they'd never seen food before.

"We'd better get in there, Al, or we won't get any!"

The two grabbed a couple of slices of pepperoni pizza, and the celebration continued. After the many speeches and congratulatory cheers, everyone started to head for home. With little room left in his stomach, Al left with a warm feeling. He knew things would finally be different.

9 780595 098767